Charlie the Chicken Finds Her Voice

By Stephen Boni
Illustrated by Maud Cronkhite

BONIFIDE BOOKS

Charlie was a happy young chicken. She loved pecking in the grass for grain. She loved laying eggs in her cozy nest. She loved clucking with her fellow chickens. But there was one thing she loved to do more than anything.

It started as something small and simple, a way to have fun while trying to lay an egg (which can be kind of boring, you know).

The more she sang, the happier she was. She especially liked to sing in the morning. It was a great way to start the day.

The other chickens did not appreciate Charlie's singing.
When she started a song, they would crowd around her and
squawk until she stopped.

"Why can't I sing? It makes me so happy," she said to the
other chickens.

"The rooster sings," they insisted. "He helps wake the
farmer and the farmhands. He's important, so you be quiet
and lay eggs like the rest of us."

There was a big problem with only the rooster being allowed to sing. His voice was . . . well . . . awful. When he sang, all the animals on the farm tried to cover their ears.

But the rooster was the rooster, and Charlie was just a chicken. What could she do? She tried to sing quietly, but it was hard to find a place where the other chickens couldn't hear her. And now she was singing so softly she could hardly hear herself.

The next morning, the rooster was at it again—singing in a squawk so sharp it made Charlie's feathers stick out.

"That's it!" she exclaimed. "I've tried to be quiet, but I will not listen to that horrible screeching anymore."

"Fine with us," said the other chickens. "You're causing a lot of problems. We're not sure we want you around this chicken coop anyway."

Charlie felt hurt. She'd lived in the chicken coop all her life. Did they truly want her to leave? "Well," she thought to herself, "at least there are a lot of places to sing on the rest of the farm."

With a sad glance behind her, Charlie stepped nervously out of the coop.

The first place Charlie visited was the pig pen. The top of the fence looked very inviting. She looked around to see if anyone was watching. All she saw were a bunch of lumps in the mud. "It looks like nobody's here," she clucked. So she hopped up and started to sing.

Charlie almost stopped singing in surprise when those muddy lumps stood up. *Pigs!*

Now, pigs like nothing better than to lie in the mud all day, and not much can get them up and moving. Today, however, the pigs just couldn't help themselves. When they heard Charlie sing, they had to get up and dance. And when Charlie saw those lumps . . . um, pigs . . . start dancing—well, that made her so happy she sang even louder.

When Charlie was done, the pigs showed her how much they liked her song by giving her hugs and claps all around. They told her to come back and sing anytime. One pig exclaimed, "There hasn't been this much excitement in the pig pen since little Squeaky was born!"

After Charlie said goodbye to the pigs, she heard a lot of noise coming from the barn. What was going on in there? It didn't sound like the rooster. She decided to investigate.

When she peeked her head in, she saw a terrible commotion. The barn cats were chasing the mice up and down the haystacks. The swallows were swooping, the barn owls were hooting like crazy, and a barnyard dog had snuck in and was chasing the cats. It was total chaos.

"I have an idea," said Charlie. She climbed to the top of the biggest haystack and started to . . .

Sing!

All the animals stopped in their tracks and became very quiet. "Who is this chicken?" they whispered to one another.

After she finished her song, Charlie said, "Now, isn't it more fun to have a little song and enjoy the day together instead of all this fussing?" Then she waved goodbye and left the barn. The animals were so amazed, they just stood around looking at one another. They didn't know what to say, but they didn't feel like fighting anymore.

Next, Charlie wandered over to look at the horses. They were big—so big that Charlie began to feel scared. But now they were looking at her. It was too late to turn back.

"H-h-h-hello," stammered Charlie. "W-w-w-would you like to hear a song?"

The horses whinnied with laughter. "You're just some little chicken," said the biggest horse.

"Yeah, chickens don't sing," added another horse.

But the smallest horse said, "Why don't we let her try?" He turned to Charlie. "We're totally bored over here, anyway, just walking around the same patch of grass all day."

Charlie took a deep breath. Her little legs were shaking, but she remembered that all the animals had enjoyed her singing so far that day (well, besides the other chickens). "I can do this," she whispered to herself. Then she said to the horses, "Maybe if I could get a little higher up, you could all hear better?"

"I don't see why not," said the biggest horse with a shrug. He stuck his head over the fence and said, "Hop on!" From the top of the horse's head, Charlie began to sing. And the other horses began to prance in delight.

A sudden noise interrupted Charlie's song. The horses stopped prancing. "Where is that coming from?" asked Charlie. "It sounds like a fiddle."

"Let's check it out," said the biggest horse. "Come on!"
And with that, he and the other horses galloped faster than
Charlie had ever seen an animal go. They were headed right
for the fence. "We're going to crash!" she thought, while
hanging on tight to the big horse's mane. With great flying
leaps, the horses sailed over the fence and landed safely on
the other side.

Charlie and the horses made their way down the path toward the sound of the music. As they rounded a bend, Charlie's feathers tingled with joy at what she saw.

A big stage was set up next to the barn. Charlie saw many of the animals she had been singing to earlier in the day. They were dancing and playing musical instruments of all kinds— not fighting or lying around bored. It was a hoedown!

All eyes turned to Charlie and her new horse friends as they approached. The pigs grinned and waved.

Just then, Charlie heard some familiar clucking and squawking. Of course, it was the rooster—strutting out in front of the pigs. The rooster shook his feathers, cleared his throat, and let out a huge screech.

Charlie couldn't let this happen. She quickly bounded onto the stage. She stood right next to the rooster and started to . . .

Sing!

All the animals began to dance. The pigs did jigs. The cats twirled on their tails. The dogs leaped and barked. The owls did acrobatics in the air. The horses pranced and stamped their hooves. Even the chickens looked happy. The rooster stopped singing and scowled. But he couldn't help tapping his toes.

Charlie was overjoyed.

After the hoedown, her fellow chickens pulled her aside.
"We were hoping you'd come back to the coop tonight.
We're so sorry we yelled at you and wouldn't let you sing.
We thought that was only a job for the rooster. But, wow,
no one even covered their ears when you sang! Maybe you
could—"

But just then, the rooster stepped forward, looking
sheepish. "Charlie, I don't want animals to cover their ears
when I sing. Would you . . . teach me?"

And Charlie, who was after all a very nice chicken, said yes.
"But," she added, "we'd better get some sleep first. We have
a lot of work to do tomorrow."

STEPHEN BONI was raised on the edge of a forest in the rocky hills of southern New Hampshire. As a child, he would often wander for hours in that forest and stumble upon crumbling old farms that had been abandoned hundreds of years before.

This was food for his vivid imagination and love of storytelling, so it was no surprise to his parents that once he was grown, he studied literature in college and film in graduate school. After years telling stories as a performance poet and creative marketing writer, Stephen was inspired by his story-loving daughter to begin writing tales for children.

Charlie the Chicken Finds Her Voice was created in conversation at the family kitchen table in Stephen's adopted home in Oakland, California, and is his first children's book.

Published by Bonifide Books, Oakland, California
www.bonifidebooks.com

Edited and designed by Girl Friday Productions
www.girlfridayproductions.com

Illustrations: Maud Cronkhite
Design: Paul Barrett
Project management: Sara Spees Addicott
Editorial: Tiffany Taing

ISBN (paperback): 978-0-578-83687-4
Library of Congress Control Number: 2021904168

CPSIA information can be obtained
at www.ICGtesting.com
Printed in the USA
BVHW020004070421
604324BV00011B/78